Star Light,
Star Bright

Hello and
Good-bye

Where
the Clouds
Go

HARCOURT BRACE JOVANOVICH, PUBLISHERS
New York Chicago San Francisco Atlanta Dallas *and* London

Hello and Good-bye

ODYSSEY An HBJ Literature Program

Sam Leaton Sebesta

Consultants

Elaine M. Aoki	Carolyn Horovitz
Willard E. Bill	Myra Cohn Livingston
Sonya Blackman	Daphne P. Muse
Sylvia Engdahl	Barre Toelken

Acknowledgments

For permission to reprint copyrighted material, grateful acknowledgment is made to the following sources:

William Cole: "Do You Know the Man?" by Shel Silverstein from *Oh, How Silly* edited by William Cole. Copyright 1970 by Shel Silverstein.

William Collins + World Publishing Co., Inc.: "Gee lee, gu lu, turn the cake" from *Chinese Mother Goose Rhymes* by Robert & Lee Wyndham. Copyright © 1968 by Robert & Lee Wyndham.

The Dial Press: A Boy, a Dog and a Frog by Mercer Mayer. Copyright © 1967 by Mercer Mayer. Reprinted by permission of The Dial Press.

Doubleday & Company, Inc.: "The Chair" from *The Collected Poems of Theodore Roethke* by Theodore Roethke. Copyright © 1950 by Theodore Roethke.

E. P. Dutton: "Happiness" from *When We Were Very Young* by A. A. Milne. Copyright 1924 by E. P. Dutton, renewal 1952 by A. A. Milne.

Four Winds Press, a division of Scholastic Magazines, Inc.: "Hopscotch" from *The Hodgepodge Book,* collected by Duncan Emrich. Text copyright © 1972 by Duncan Emrich. "Four legs up and four legs down" from *The Nonsense Book* by Duncan Emrich. Text copyright © 1970 by Duncan Emrich.

Harcourt Brace Jovanovich, Inc.: "An old silent pond" by Basho from *Cricket Songs: Japanese Haiku,* translated by Harry Behn, © 1964 by Harry Behn. "Understanding" from *The Moon and a Star* by Myra Cohn Livingston, © 1965 by Myra Cohn Livingston.

Holt, Rinehart and Winston, Publishers: "One, two, three, a-lary" from *A Rocket in My Pocket* compiled by Carl Withers. Copyright 1948 by Carl Withers. Copyright © 1976 by Samuel H. Halperin.

Houghton Mifflin Company and The Macmillan Company of Canada Limited: "Skyscraper" from *Alligator Pie* by Dennis Lee. Copyright © 1974 by Dennis Lee.

J. B. Lippincott Company: "Some people I know" from *Only the Moon and Me* by Richard J. Margolis. Copyright © 1969 by Richard J. Margolis.

Little, Brown and Company: "Bananas and Cream" from *Take Sky: More Rhymes of the Never Was and Always Is* by David McCord. Copyright © 1961, 1962 by David McCord. "Higglety, pigglety, pop!" from *Granfa' Grig Had a Pig* compiled and illustrated by Wallace Tripp.

Macmillan Publishing Co., Inc.: "Mix a pancake" from *Sing-Song* by Christina G. Rossetti. Macmillan Publishing Co., Inc., 1924. *The Chick and the Duckling* by Mirra Ginsburg, illustrated by Jose Aruego. Copyright © 1972 Mirra Ginsburg. Copyright © 1972 Jose Aruego.

Margit W. MacRae: "Uno, dos, tres, cho-" from *Teaching Spanish in the Grades* by Margit W. MacRae. Copyright © 1957 by Houghton Mifflin Company.

Edward B. Marks Music Corporation: "Barnyard Song" from *Songs to Grow On* edited by Beatrice Landeck. © Copyright: Edward B. Marks Music Corporation.

National Textbook Company: "Qué es aquello" and "What is it that stands?" from *Mother Goose on the Rio Grande* by Frances Alexander. Copyright © 1973 by National Textbook Company.

Oxford University Press: "One, two, three, four, five" from *The Oxford English Dictionary of Nursery Rhymes* by Iona and Peter Opie, 1951.

G. P. Putnam's Sons: "After Supper" from *Here, There, and Everywhere* by Dorothy Aldis. Copyright 1927, 1928 by Dorothy Aldis.

Random House, Inc.: "Green cheese, yellow laces" from *The Mother Goose Book* by Alice and Martin Provensen. Copyright © 1976 by Alice and Martin Provensen.

Russell & Volkening, Inc. as agents for the author: "Hello and Good-bye" by Mary Ann Hoberman. Copyright © 1959 by Mary Ann Hoberman.

Schroder Music Company: From the song "I Live in a City" from *Tweedles and Foodles for Young Noodles,* words and music by Malvina Reynolds. Copyright 1960 by Schroder Music Company. (ASCAP).

Western Publishing Company, Inc.: "The Gingerbread Boy" adapted from *The Tall Book of Nursery Tales.* Copyright © 1944 by Western Publishing Company, Inc.

Art Acknowledgments

Ronni Shepherd: 69.

Cover: Richard Brown.

Contents

To Market, to Market   A Mother Goose rhyme   *8*

Green Cheese, Yellow Laces   An old rhyme   *10*

A Boy, a Dog, and a Frog
   A story in pictures by Mercer Mayer   *12*

An old silent pond   A haiku by Basho   *19*

Mix a Pancake   A poem by Christina Rossetti   *20*

Bananas and Cream   From a poem by David McCord   *22*

Uno, Dos, Tres, Cho—   A Mexican counting rhyme   *24*

One, Two, Three, Four, Five   An old counting rhyme   *26*

The Three Bears
   An English folk tale retold in pictures   *30*

LEARN ABOUT STORIES: **Story Places, Story Faces**   *44*

The Chair   A poem by Theodore Roethke   *46*

Some People I Know   A poem by Richard J. Margolis   *47*

After Supper   A poem by Dorothy Aldis   *48*

The Chick and the Duckling
   From a story by Vladimir Suteyev   *50*

Barnyard Song   A Kentucky folk song   *70*

LEARN ABOUT THE LIBRARY:

Rabbit Gets a Library Book *76*

I Live in a City From a song by Malvina Reynolds *80*

Skyscraper A poem by Dennis Lee *82*

One, Two, Three, A-lary A rhyme *84*

Hopscotch A rhyme *86*

Gee Lee, Gu Lu An old Chinese rhyme *87*

The Gingerbread Man

A play based on an American folk tale *88*

LEARN ABOUT STORIES: Story Mix-Up *110*

What Is It? Two riddles *112*

Hickory, Dickory, Dock A Mother Goose rhyme *114*

Higglety, Pigglety, Pop An old rhyme *116*

Do You Know the Man? A poem by Shel Silverstein *118*

Understanding A poem by Myra Cohn Livingston *120*

Hello and Good-bye

A poem by Mary Ann Hoberman *122*

Happiness A poem by A. A. Milne *128*

To Market, To Market

A Mother Goose rhyme

To market, to market,
　　To buy a fat pig,
Home again, home again,
　　Jiggety-jig.
To market, to market,
　　To buy a fat hog,
Home again, home again,
　　Jiggety-jog.

8　　　　　　　Picture by Tony Kenyon

Green Cheese, Yellow Laces

An old rhyme

Green cheese,
Yellow laces,
Up and down
The market places.

Picture by Tony Kenyon

11

A BOY, A DOG, and A FROG

A picture story by Mercer Mayer

1

2

3

4

5

6

7

8

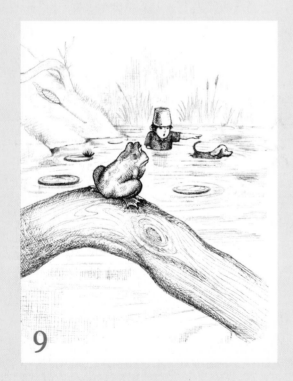

9

10

11

12

13

16

16

17

18

19

20

21

An old silent pond . . .
A frog jumps into the pond,
splash! Silence again.

A Japanese haiku by Basho

Mix a Pancake

A poem by Christina Rossetti

Mix a pancake,
Stir a pancake,
   Pop it in the pan;
Fry the pancake,
Toss the pancake,—
   Catch it if you can.

Pictures by Marie-Louise Gay

Bananas and Cream

From a poem by David McCord

Bananas and cream,
Bananas and cream,
All we could say was
Bananas and cream.

We couldn't say fruit,
We wouldn't say cow,
We didn't say sugar—
We don't say it now.

Picture by Sharon Harker

Bananas and cream,

Bananas and cream,

All we could shout was

BANANAS AND CREAM.

Uno, Dos, Tres, Cho-

A Mexican counting rhyme

Uno, dos, tres, **cho-**

Uno, dos, tres, **co-**

Uno, dos, tres, **la-**

Uno, dos, tres, **te**.

Chocolate, chocolate,

¡bate, bate, el **chocolate!**

One, Two, Three, Four, Five

An old counting rhyme

One, two, three, four, five,

I caught a fish alive,

Pictures by Dennis Ziemienski

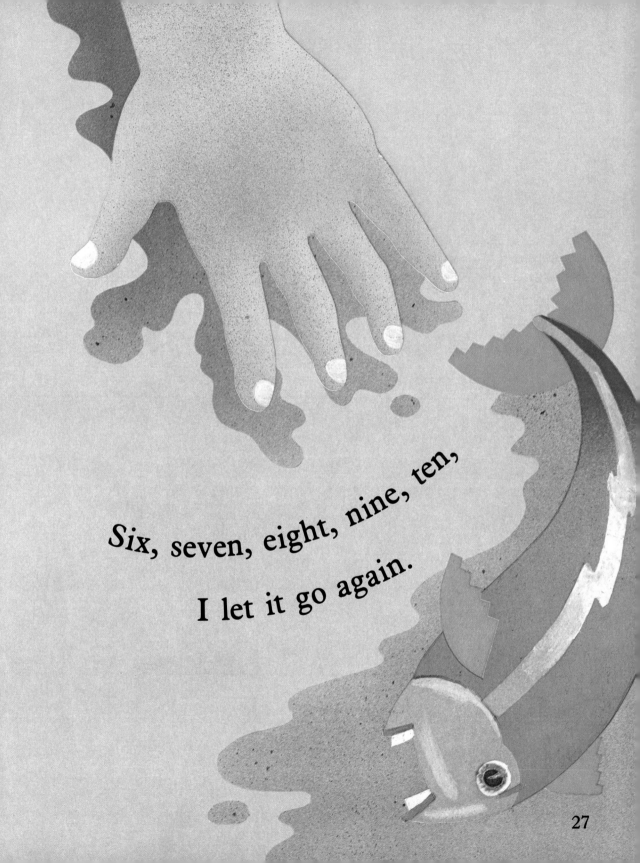

Six, seven, eight, nine, ten,

I let it go again.

Why did you let it go?
Because it bit my finger so.

Which finger did it bite?
This little finger on the right.

THE THREE BEARS

An English folk tale retold in pictures by Kinuko Craft

This porridge is too hot.

Let us go for a walk.
When we come back,
our porridge will be ready
to eat.

Somebody has been sitting
in my chair—
and has sat the bottom out!

Somebody has been lying
in my bed—
and here she is!

Story Places, Story Faces

In each place along the road,
You'll find something wrong.
Tell who *should* be in each place
As you go along.

START

Grandma's House

Mr. McGregor's Garden

Little Boy Blue's Haystack

Little Miss Muffet's Tuffet

The Witch's Gingerbread House

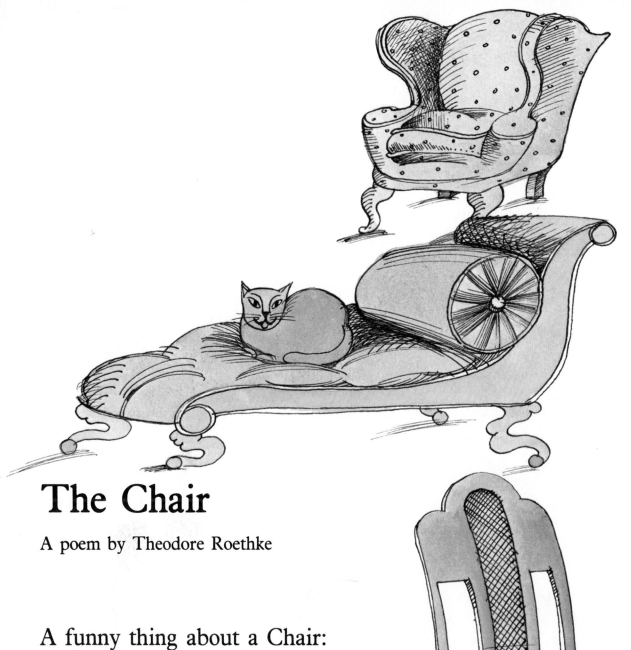

The Chair

A poem by Theodore Roethke

A funny thing about a Chair:
You hardly ever think it's *there*.
To know a Chair is really it,
You sometimes have to go and sit.

Picture by Roseanne Litzinger

Some People I Know

A poem by Richard J. Margolis

Some people I know
fill up the whole chair.
They don't share.

After Supper

A poem by Dorothy Aldis

Let's not pretend we're anywhere;
Let's only sit here in this chair.

I don't want to play that we
Are sailors sailing on the sea,
Or pirates in a pirates' cave
Or even lions being brave.

I'm feeling very nice and near.
Let's just be here.

Picture by Charles Robinson

The Chick and the Duckling

A story by Vladimir Suteyev

Translated from the Russian by Mirra Ginsburg

Pictures by Jose and Ariane Aruego

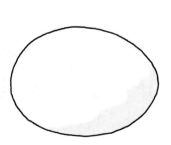

A Duckling came out
of the shell.
"I am out!" the Duckling said.

"Me too," said the Chick.

"I am taking a walk,"
said the Duckling.

"Me too,"
said the Chick.

"I am digging a hole,"
said the Duckling.

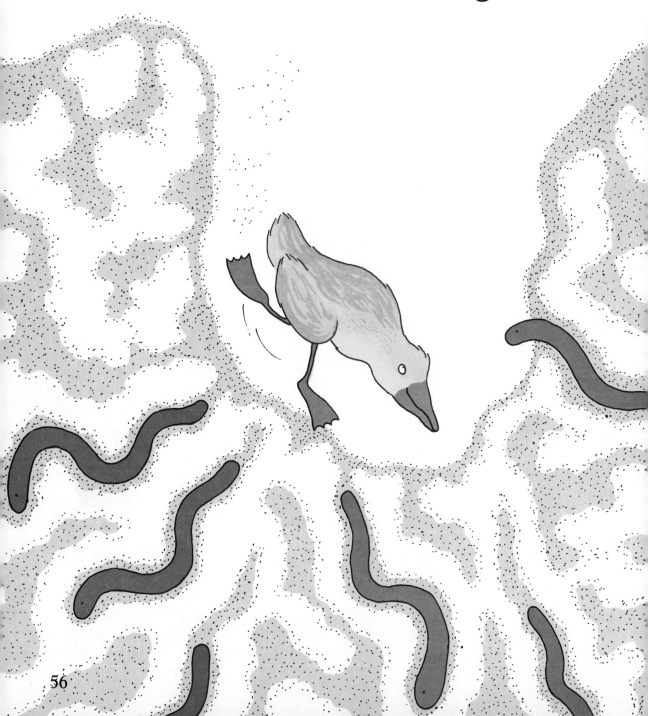

"Me too,"
said the Chick.

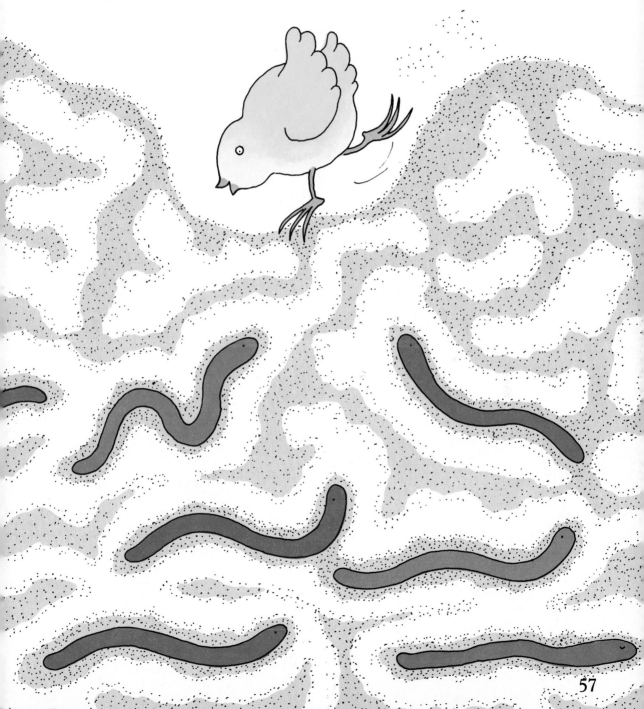

"I have found a worm,"
said the Duckling.

"Me too,"
said the Chick.

"I am swimming,"
said the Duckling.

"Me too!"
said the Chick.

The Duckling pulled
the Chick out.

"I am going for another swim," said the Duckling.

"Not me,"
said the Chick.

Questions

1. What did the Chick do well?

walk   swim   dig

2. What will the fox say?

     Me too.

     Not me.

3. What will the girl say?

     Me too.

     Not me.

Activity

What can you do well?

Draw or paint a picture to show your answer.

Barnyard Song

A Kentucky folk song

I had a cat, and the cat pleased me,

I fed my cat under yonder tree.

Cat goes fiddle dee dee.

Pictures by Marie-Louise Gay

I had a hen, and the hen pleased me,
I fed my hen under yonder tree.
Hen goes chimmy chuck, chimmy chuck,
Cat goes fiddle dee dee.

I had a duck, and the duck pleased me,
I fed my duck under yonder tree.
Duck goes quack, quack,
Hen goes chimmy chuck, chimmy chuck,
Cat goes fiddle dee dee.

I had a cow, and the cow pleased me,

I fed my cow under yonder tree.

Cow goes moo, moo,

Duck goes quack, quack,

Hen goes chimmy chuck, chimmy chuck,

Cat goes fiddle dee dee.

Rabbit Gets a Library Book

Pictures by Ed Taber

2 Do you like funny stories?

I like funny animal stories.

3 Here's a funny animal story. I think you'll like it.

HARRY by the sea

4 Have you read this book?

Yes. It's very funny.

HARRY by the sea

5 I like the part where Harry looks like a sea monster. Ha, Ha, Ha.

6

This is the book I want.

7

Bring the book back on this day. Then you can pick out another book.

8

HOME SWEET HUTCH

Library Books

Ha, Ha, Ha.

9

Good. You brought your book back on time. Did you like it?

Yes. Do you have any more stories about Harry?

I Live in a City

A song by Malvina Reynolds

I live in a city,
Yes I do,
I live in a city,
Yes I do,
I live in a city,
Yes I do,
Made by human hands.

Picture by Ted Carr

Skyscraper

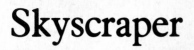

A poem by Dennis Lee

Skyscraper, skyscraper,
Scrape me some sky,
Tickle the sun
While the stars go by.

Tickle the stars
While the sun's climbing high,
Then skyscraper, skyscraper
Scrape me some sky.

Pictures by Charles Robinson

One, Two, Three, A-lary

A jump-rope rhyme

One, two, three, a-lary
My first name is Mary;
If you think it's necessary,
Find it in the dictionary.

Picture by Linda Boehm Weller

85

Hopscotch

A rhyme

Hopscotch, let us hop,

Hopscotch, let us stop,

Let us hop, then you stop,

Let us stop, then you hop,

Hopscotch, hopscotch,

Let   us   hop!

Picture by Linda Boehm Weller

Gee Lee, Gu Lu

An old Chinese rhyme

Gee lee, gu lu, turn the cake,
Add some oil, the better to bake.

Gee lee, gu lu, now it's done;
Give a piece to everyone.

The Gingerbread Man

A play adapted from the American folk tale

Pictures by Willi Baum

Characters

Storyteller 1	**Little Old Woman**	**Cow**
Storyteller 2	**Little Old Man**	**Bear**
Storyteller 3	**Gingerbread Man**	**Fox**

Storyteller 1: Once upon a time
a little old woman
and a little old man
lived in a little old house.
They were very happy,
but they had no children.
They wanted a child
of their own.

Storyteller 2: One day the little old woman
was making gingerbread.
She laughed and said,

Little Old Woman: I'll make us a son
out of gingerbread!

Storyteller 3: So she rolled out the dough,
and she cut out a man.
She gave him raisin eyes,
a raisin mouth,
and a coat with raisin buttons.
Then she popped him
into the oven.

Storyteller 1: Before long,
the little old woman looked
to see if the gingerbread man
was done.

Storyteller 2: As soon as the oven door
was opened,
out he jumped!
Off he ran,
out the door,
and down the road.

Little Old Woman: Come back! Come back!

Storyteller 3: Called the little old woman.

Little Old Man: Come back! Come back!

Storyteller 1: Called the little old man.

Storyteller 2: But the gingerbread man
only laughed and said,

Gingerbread Man: Run, run, as fast as you can.
You can't catch me!
I'm the gingerbread man!

Storyteller 3: The little old woman
and the little old man
ran after him.
But they couldn't catch him.

Storyteller 1: A cow looked up
as the gingerbread man
ran by.
She called,

Cow: Come back! Come back!

Storyteller 2: But the gingerbread man
only laughed and said,

Gingerbread Man: Run, run, as fast as you can.
You can't catch me!
I'm the gingerbread man!
I've run away
From a little old woman,
And a little old man,
And I can run away
From you, too.
I can, I can!

Storyteller 3: The cow ran after
the gingerbread man.
But she couldn't catch him.

Storyteller 1: A bear was looking
for something to eat.
Just then,
the gingerbread man ran by.
The bear called,

Bear: Come back! Come back!

Storyteller 2: But the gingerbread man
only laughed and said,

Gingerbread Man: Run, run, as fast as you can.
You can't catch me!
I'm the gingerbread man!
I've run away
From a little old woman,
And a little old man,
And a cow.
And I can run away
From you, too.
I can, I can!

Storyteller 3: The bear ran after
the gingerbread man.
But he couldn't catch him.

Storyteller 1: Down by the river was a fox.
Along ran the gingerbread man,
saying,

Gingerbread Man: Run, run, as fast as you can.
You can't catch me!
I'm the gingerbread man!
I've run away
From a little old woman,
And a little old man,
And a cow,
And a bear.
And I can run away
From you, too.
I can, I can!

Storyteller 2: But the fox
did not run after him.
She just said sweetly,

Fox: I don't want to catch you,
gingerbread man.
But if you hop on my tail,
I will give you a ride
across the river.

Storyteller 3: The gingerbread man hopped
onto the fox's tail.
And they started
across the river.

Storyteller 1: When the water got deeper, the fox called out,

Fox: Hop on my back or you will get wet.

Storyteller 2: So the gingerbread man hopped onto the fox's back.

Storyteller 3: When the water got deeper,
the fox called out,

Fox: Hop on my head
or you will get wet.

Storyteller 1: So the gingerbread man
hopped onto the fox's head.

Storyteller 2: Suddenly
the fox tossed back her head
and opened her mouth.

Storyteller 3: And that was the end
of the gingerbread man
and the end
of this story, too.

Questions

Bear

Fox

Cow

Gingerbread Man

Pig

Little Old Man
and Little Old Woman

1. Who ran after me first?

2. Who ran after me next?

3. Who ran after me then?

4. Who gave me a ride?

5. Who didn't get away from me?

swim   jump   walk   talk   run   laugh

6.  What can I do?

7.  What *can't* I do?

Activity

The little old woman baked something new.

What did she bake?

What happened then?

Story Mix-up

In each story, you will see,

There is a mix-up

That you need to fix up.

Which pictures are 1, 2, and 3?

Pictures by Ed Taber

What Is It?

¿Qué es aquello
que colgado en la pared
da sin tener manos
y anda sin tener pies?

(El reloj.)

What is it that stands
  Or hangs on the wall,
Runs fast with its hands,
  Has no feet at all?

(A clock.)

—A Mexican riddle

Four legs up and four legs down,
Soft in the middle and hard all around.

(A bed.)

—An old American riddle

Hickory, Dickory, Dock

A Mother Goose Rhyme

Hickory, dickory, dock,
The mouse ran up the clock.
    The clock struck one.
    The mouse ran down,
Hickory, dickory, dock.

Picture by Sharon Harker

BONG

Higglety, Pigglety, Pop

An old rhyme

Higglety, pigglety, pop!
The dog has eaten the mop;
The pig's in a hurry,
The cat's in a flurry,

Pictures by Tony Kenyon

Higglety, pigglety, **pop!**

Do You Know the Man?

A poem by Shel Silverstein

Do you know the man with the flowers growing

Out of the top of his head?

Yellow flowers,

Purple flowers,

Orange, green, and red.

Growing there

Just like hair

Out of the top of his head.

(Yes, you heard just what I said—

Out of the top of his head.)

118

Picture by Tony Kenyon

Understanding

A poem by Myra Cohn Livingston

Sun
and rain
and wind
and storms
and thunder go together.

There has to be a little bit of each
to make the
weather.

Hello and Good-bye

A poem by Mary Ann Hoberman

Hello and good-bye
Hello and good-bye

When I'm in a swing
Swinging low and then high
Good-bye to the ground
Hello to the sky.

Pictures by Stan Tusan

Hello to the rain
Good-bye to the sun,
Then hello again sun
When the rain is all done.

In blows the winter,
Away the birds fly.
Good-bye and hello
Hello and good-bye.

127

Happiness

A poem by A. A. Milne

John had
Great Big
Waterproof
Boots on;
John had a
Great Big
Waterproof
Hat;
John had a
Great Big
Waterproof
Mackintosh—
And **that**
(Said John)
Is
That.

128   Picture by Stan Tusan